Once Upon a Wintry Krampusnacht Eve

Bernie Mojzes

NE●PARADOXA

Pennsville, NJ

PUBLISHED BY
NeoParadoxa,
a division of eSpec Books LLC
Danielle McPhail,
Publisher
PO Box 242,
Pennsville, New Jersey 08070
www.especbooks.com

ISBN: 978-1-965266-27-4
ISBN (ebook): 978-1-965266-26-7

Cover and Interior Design: Danielle McPhail, McP Digital Graphics

To Mom & Dad
who took me to Mondsee one
wintry Krampusnacht

Author's Note

MONDSEE IS A REAL TOWN, AND IT'S REALLY IN AUSTRIA. IT REALLY IS on a lake that perfectly reflects the moon, surrounded by treacherous mountains. It really has a church that is over 1200 years old, and a market plaza called Marktplatz. And it really has a Krampusnacht celebration in the Marktplatz, in front of the older-than-ancient church. There are videos of it online. It's very sweet and tame, considering, and there's even a benevolent St. Nikolaus who presides over the whole thing.

It's not the same event that I remember.

When I was about Mia's age, well before the Internet and online videos — or even video tape recorders — were invented, we spent half a year in Europe, and as winter settled in, we ended up staying in a building that had been intended as a retreat for theology students, about as high up on the side of the mountain as the road went. The clouds, the cows, the dairy farm, the switchback roads, that was all my life for a few months.

And Krampusnacht was not sweet, and it was not tame.

It was terror. And pain. It was whips, and monsters, and horses' hooves sparking on the cobblestones next to your head.

It was parents pushing crying children into reach of the Krampus's whips and cheering them on.

And all the coins and candy you dared to grab.

It's a night that's indelibly imprinted on my soul. I hope, after you've read this, a little bit is imprinted on yours, too.

Chapter 1
Krampusnacht

TRUTH TOLD, MIA HAD NEVER BEEN A GOOD CHILD. I MEAN, SHE wasn't evil, per se. Just mischievous, obstinate, combative, and generally difficult. She had entered the "No!" and "Why?" phases of development at the expected time, then never grew out of them. Instead, she just collected all these infuriating behaviors and created ever-more-clever combinations to drive her mother and me insane. "Why?" was almost inevitably followed by a lengthy series of additional "why?"s as she challenged our — and everyone else's — intentions, which she almost inevitably found unconvincing.

"No," of course, gradually gained sophistication. Became "Sounds dumb." Or "Boring." Or a snooty "I think not" after she discovered British television. Or just an eyeroll and a puff of air.

By the middle of Mia's eleventh year, we were terrified of what twelve would bring, never mind her teens. Hopefully, she wouldn't forget her "No"s when it came to boys. Or girls. Whatever happened there would come as a surprise to us; if Mia had any sense of romance in her heart, she had successfully hidden it from her parents and manipulated any attempt at the birds-and-bees conversation into uncomfortably precise interrogations regarding our own particular practices.

The Internet did not make parenting easier. I didn't know whether to be dismayed or proud of how easily Mia circumvented so-called "parental controls." Proud, probably. Someday. If we all survived that long.

So, in hindsight, maybe none of this should have surprised us.

Mia's "no" reflex geared into overdrive for this entire trip. Right from the start, she'd rejected the very idea when Laura got the offer to teach a semester abroad at the Universität Mozarteum Salzburg. In Salzburg. Austria.

"Sixth grade is a very important milestone in a student's education," she said. "You two go, I can take care of myself." And "Who's going to feed my snake?" And "You can't just put Toby in a kennel for half a year!"

Toby was our God-only-knows-what-his-mom-took-up-with five-year-old puppy, who was not going near a kennel. Toby got along well with my brother's dogs, and my only worry was that he wouldn't want to come back to us when we returned.

Honestly, I was more concerned about what this trip would mean for my own foundering career than I was about the fate of Mia's menagerie. Mia was too young to reasonably expect to notice, but I found Laura's indifference hurtful. Yes, the loss of my income would hardly make a dent in the household budget, but that didn't make me superfluous, did it?

We almost missed our flight because Mia disappeared into the woods behind our house the night before. The police found her running around the railroad tracks the next day, frantically searching for her pet garter snake, which she'd taken with her. She'd put it on a rock to warm up in the morning sun and it had taken the opportunity to gain its freedom.

Once we were in Salzburg, she settled in just fine, wandering the university halls, "playing" the pianos in the practice rooms, and befriending all the students while simultaneously making enemies of all the professors. So, when we announced we were going to spend a weekend in Mondsee for Krampusnacht, she reflexively argued against it.

Krampusnacht, we explained, was an Alpine celebration of the dreaded Krampus, St. Nick's demonic helper who punished all the bad kids so Santa could concentrate on giving gifts to the good children. And Mondsee was one of the towns and villages that still celebrated in a traditional manner.

"It's like Halloween and Christmas all mashed together," I said. Mia had been bitter about missing Halloween back home, so I had hoped this might placate her.

"So, you think we should just nose in?" Mia said. "Talk about cultural appropriation!"

"You're just scared the Krampus is going to get you," Laura said.

"No, I'm not! I'm just..." Mia searched for the right words.

"Culturally sensitive?" I offered.

"Yeah!"

"That'll be the day," Laura scoffed, with good reason. Mia was the verbal equivalent of a bull in a china shop, blurting out whatever thought was on the tip of her brain without consideration of what people around her might think or feel.

"I'll stay with Leopold," she declared. Leopold was one of Laura's students, and a talented oboe player. Mia, who had shown absolutely no interest in music when Laura tried to engage her, was now taking lessons from him. We'd worried at how close they'd become in such a short time, until we learned that he was both gay and ace, and had an aversion to even modest physical contact with anyone.

"You can't stay with Leopold. He'd get kicked out of the college."

"But if I explain..."

"If you explain, I'm sure it'll be even worse."

And of course, the conversation devolved from there, ending up having nothing whatsoever to do with our plans to visit Mondsee for the Krampusnacht festival.

Once, Laura and I took Mia to Independence Hall in Philadelphia. Afterward, we took a tour in a horse carriage, sharing the ride with an older German couple. The tour guide informed us that Elfreth's Alley is the oldest residential street in America, with houses dating back to 1720. One of the Germans said something to the other, and they both laughed. Laura laughed, too—a side-effect of obsessively studying Mozart was learning the language (which ultimately resulted with us being in Austria, and worse).

"What's so funny?" Mia demanded.

One German woman pointed at Elfreth's Alley and said, "New construction."

The other German woman said, "Our doorstep is older."

Mondsee is everything you'd expect from a Modern Medieval Alpine town. Central to the town is Mondsee Abbey, which was founded in the year 748 on the ruins of an even older Roman settlement. The abbey was now the Basilica of St. Michael and had been extensively rebuilt over the centuries, but the bell tower that rose above the rest of the town still evoked a sense of immense age and gravity that the local people seemed entirely oblivious of or immune to.

In front of the church was the Marktplatz, the town square, which was paved in a confusing combination of cobblestone, flagstone, and marble tiles. Even in the chill of early December it was cheery — the church and its adjacent buildings painted a pleasant buttercup yellow, while the sturdy buildings surrounding the Marktplatz adopted a variety of complementary pastel shades. Gift shops and bars and restaurants and hairdressers and watch shops vied for attention, all in a discreet and genteel manner. A quiet beckon: *Look, here is a lovely place that you may find to your liking in amongst all these other lovely places.* No neon, nothing that *shouted*, visually speaking.

Elsewhere in Mondsee there was a McDonald's, which looked just as you might expect. When Mia saw it on the maps app, she forced us to go, and then complained that the burgers and the Coke both tasted weird. But that was in a newer part of town.

We had taken a room in a Gasthaus on Mondseeberg. Moon-lake mountain. The drive was longer than we expected in our underpowered rental car, up steep inclines and around sharp switchbacks. The Gasthaus was the second-to-last building before the road ended. Up the road there was only a dairy farm. The improbable fields of hardy mountain grasses that surrounded the Gasthaus seemed better suited for mountain goats than dairy cows, but the cows made it work, miraculously not rolling down into the lake. This high up, snow had collected in shady patches, on the road and in the fields, under trees and beside boulders. It seemed a good place to see for ourselves the phenomenon that the town (Mondsee) and the lake (Mondsee) were named for. And sure enough, as dusk began to fall, the full moon reflected perfectly on the dark, motionless surface of the lake.

"Imagine what this looked like before electric lights and car headlights," Laura said.

"Why?" Mia responded.

"Because I said so," I grumbled.

Mia frowned at me. "But you didn't say it."

And if we could have pulled it off, I think Laura and I would have replied to the contrary in unison, but we weren't that good.

The morning dawned bright and glorious and shone like gold through the curtains. Below us, the lake, the town, the base of the mountain, everything was gone, replaced with a sea of white, fluffy clouds. As the morning warmed, the clouds climbed the mountain and suddenly, we were in the midst of them. The air, which had been both brisk and sun-warmed, turned suddenly wet and chill and dark, the fog so thick I couldn't see my hand if I stretched my arm out in front of me.

Mia vanished, of course, into the pea-soup fog, and we had only vaguest idea where she was from the giggles, the thumps and splashes, the shriek when she discovered the electric fence that kept the cows from wandering. Adorable little eleven-year-old curses — *Ow! Oh, shoot! Motherlover!*

"Kid's going to be a terror," I grumbled.

"Going to be?"

The fog lifted into a dense cloud cover, and we were finally able to see Mia. She'd managed to get through the electric fence and was trying to pet one of the cows, which made a point of not being petted.

After she escaped the bull that decided to defend Mia's cow, she returned to us, shivering and soaked to the bone, having waded through — or fallen into — snow and slush and mud and cow pies, and by the time we got her into the shower and cleaned up, the clouds had dissolved and we were back into brilliant glory.

Her clothes were another matter.

"Do we burn them now?" Laura asked. "Or burn them back in Salzburg?"

As bright and cheery as the Mondsee Marktplatz was by day, it was something else on a cold December night. The air had tasted of snow, and occasionally there'd be a brief flurry. I hoped it didn't start snowing for real, or we might never make it back up the mountain in our little rental car. But it was Krampusnacht in Mondsee, and this is what we had come to see.

Of course, Mia had argued. It was stupid. It was too cold and why couldn't we just watch TV? Besides, Krampus was heathen and we were all going to go to hell.

Laura and I looked at each other.

"We heathens don't have hell," Laura said.

"That's not what Carly says!"

Carly was a school friend of Mia's. They'd been emailing and video chatting a lot since we'd left for Europe. Carly's mom's new boyfriend, we knew, asserted certain delusions, and now it appeared he had not only corrupted Carly, but was using her to exert influence on her friends. We might need to stage an intervention. When we got home.

"Your mom's right, Mia. Heathens don't go to hell. Neither do pagans, Wiccans, or persons of other non-Abrahamic faiths."

"Where do you go, then?"

"Ohio," Laura said.

"Mondsee," Mia snarled.

"Put your coat on," I suggested, "or you're gonna get real cold."

We'd had to park some distance away from the Marktplatz and make our way there on foot. It wasn't quite dark yet, but it was cold. The sky hung gray and heavy over both town and lake. What little snow fell collected on the edges of the street and sidewalks where the wind and passersby blew it. Mia made a point of walking on it wherever it collected enough to do so, grinning at the crunch of it under her boots.

I'm trying to remember the last time we had a good cold-enough-to-crunch snow back home. All we've gotten lately is heavy, wet snow that's half slush by the time I get out with a shovel. I guess this was new experience territory for Mia, so I couldn't really blame her.

A crowd had gathered in the Marktplatz. Someone had set up giant torches around the square, making a sort of amoeba-like circle. People milled around the outside of the circle, more or less, the adults in various states of inebriation. Those who hadn't brought their own flasks were drinking a dubious-looking beverage purchased from a dubious-looking street vendor. The heavily enriched mulled wine that tasted like hangovers.

Meanwhile, the children waited, pensive and nervous. There was a band playing some sort of traditional-sounding folk music, off-key demented polkas, with sleigh bell embellishments.

"Diminished fifth?" Laura wrinkled her nose. "Ugh. Locrian."

I have no idea how the tuba player's lips didn't freeze to the mouthpiece. We kept warm by buying and eating several bags of roasted chestnuts.

As the last light faded, the band grew quiet, and so did the crowd, insofar as a crowd of drunk parents can be quiet.

Then we heard them.

Galloping horses are loud. Put them on cobblestone streets, surrounded by buildings that echo and magnify the sharp, thunderous, ringing sounds—then turn out the lights—and it's terrifying.

The ground vibrated under our feet.

The crowd cheered as the horses thundered around the corner, the torchlight casting looming shadows of the monstrous beasts on their backs. Cheering that broke in confusion as the horses and their riders crashed through the mass of people, somehow miraculously not trampling anyone. One of them came straight toward us. I was just barely able to pull Mia and myself out of harm's way, crying out for Laura, whom I expected to see lying broken on the ground. She wasn't.

She was grinning. "These guys really know how to ride!"

That much became evident as they filled the torchlit circle with bucking and rearing beast flesh and menacing shadows. Each of the riders was fully costumed—long, shaggy fur covering their entire bodies, massive horns or antlers (Laura and I argued about which, until other things became more important), and twisted, demonic faces. Each one unique. Different horns, different color and texture fur, different faces and expressions. All of them horrifying.

Each of the Krampuses—Krampi? (Another marital debate, again, until we had more pressing concerns)—carried with them three things: a flask (which they partook of regularly), an instrument of torture (either a long birch switch or a horsehair whip), and a bulging burlap sack. They growled and roared and cackled as they drove their horses into a frenzy while cracking their whips into the air.

Meanwhile, the band had swapped their regular instruments for something new—improvised percussion, trays of sheet metal that they struck with sticks and metal rattles that sounded like the chains of Marley's ghost. The evening had gone from a quaint-if-spooky Alpine festival to something far more primal. The Krampuses and their horses all bore massive sleigh bells that crashed more than they jingled—in time with the clatter of the horses' hooves, but out of time with the band—to cacophonous effect.

Nervously, the town's children edged up to the "circle" defined by the torches. They ranged from teens a few years older than Mia but not yet too cool for this foolishness, all the way down to toddlers. Some of the kids needed prodding, and some of the parents had to accompany their crying children.

Mia exhaled a dismissive consonant between her teeth and crossed her arms.

"Go on," Laura urged. "Join the other kids. This is when it gets exciting."

"I think not."

"I'll hold your hand if you're too scared," I said.

"I'm not scared!"

I quoted Mia's dismissive consonant.

"I'm *not!*"

Mia slapped my hand away and joined the other children, pushing to the front of the group. Glancing back at us to make sure we were watching her not being scared.

And then it was our turn to be scared.

The men in the Krampus costumes settled their horses, and then in unison, began flinging handfuls out of their burlap sacks. Copper and silver flashed in the torchlight, coins that tinkled as they struck the cobblestones and bounced or rolled. Hard candies and chocolates scattered across the Marktplatz.

With a cheer that sounded suspiciously like a terrified bleat, the children surged forward, grabbing at the bounty in front of them and stuffing everything they could get a hold of into their pockets. The older kids made their way right to the middle of the fray, where there was less competition from the smaller kids. Mia, of course, was right there with them.

And then the beatings began. With the children crawling around beneath the flashing hooves, the Krampuses (Krampi?) began whipping the children, a sharp slap of the switch across a reaching hand, a whip across the bottom. They were merciless. The children screamed and cried and kept scrambling for more coins, more candy, heedless of the pain, or of the risk of having their skulls caved in by a stray horse hoof.

It was madness, and I think both Laura and I were regretting our choice to come here. We should have gone to a less traditional celebration, one where there was a Saint Nick to keep the Krampuses in line, and nobody actually whipped anyone in a non-consensual way.

Still, by some miracle of Krampusnacht, nobody died. Nobody lost an eye, or had any body parts crushed under a horse's hoof. And I suppose things might have been okay if Mia hadn't decided she was tired of getting hit.

She abandoned her quest for riches and stood up tall.

"Hey!" she shouted. "Cut it out! I've had it up to here—"

Just as Laura was giving me her patented I-wonder-where-she-got-that-line-from look, the Krampus Mia was facing slashed out with his switch and struck her in the face. Her head snapped back. Already there was an angry red stripe from her ear to her chin, across her bleeding lips. An inch higher and it would have taken her eye.

While I was staring in shock at my daughter staring in shock, Laura was already moving, shoving past parents and kids and horses alike to confront the man who'd assaulted her child. She started screaming at him—it was in German so I couldn't tell you exactly what, but the Krampus just laughed.

With a flick of his wrist, he struck Laura across the chest, and then again and again until she got her arms up in front of her. When she still didn't back down, he urged his horse toward her.

My brain and body finally figured out that we needed to do something, so I ran up to join Laura. Exactly what the two of us could do against a man with a whip on horseback, I had no idea, but apparently when his attempt at intimidation failed, he turned away, toward the other kids, and started throwing more coins and candy out into the crowd.

I exhaled in relief and hugged Laura, and then we turned to collect Mia and go home.

And this is where all the fears we never even knew to fear came true.

"Come on, honey, let's go home," Laura was saying.

Mia was already heading toward us, not running, because that's something a *child* would do, but she was going to be *twelve* in a few months, and hardly a child anymore, and she wasn't going run any more than she was going to cry.

And that meant that she didn't see the thing metamorphosing behind her. What had been a normal man-sized Krampus on a normal-sized horse was changing shape, horse and rider melting together, merging into something so much more horrible than any costume could ever mimic. This new Krampus of many limbs and weirdly undulating flesh would have stood a good eight feet tall, if it stood to its full height. Instead, it crouched and skittered, almost insect-like, until it was directly behind Mia.

"Mia! Run!"

Laura screamed. I screamed. *We* screamed as we ran toward her. Toward the monster.

Mia didn't run. She turned around. She took one step backward.

It pounced.

Four limbs reached out and snatched her up, pulling her tight against its body.

Mia screamed.

I'd never heard Mia scream before. Mia didn't scream. Hadn't since she was a baby. But now she screamed. I felt like I was going to die from the sound of it.

The Krampus turned away from us, crouching lower on its four other limbs, which looked like some combination of horse, human, and spider legs.

Laura and I leapt on it, grabbing hold of its thick fur. I wasn't sure what we could do from here. I could punch it in the kidney. If it had kidneys. Maybe I could climb up its back and gouge its eyes out.

But before we could figure that out, it leapt.

Chapter 2
Endless Nacht

THE KRAMPUS LEAPT A LONG WAY, AND FOR A LONG TIME. IT FELT like we were skimming the surface of things, though what things those were was a mystery.

I hung on for dear life and prayed Laura didn't lose her grip. There was no way I could even attempt to try to support her, not without losing my own grip and sending us both tumbling. At the speed we were traveling, there's no guarantee either of us would survive, but even if we did, we'd never see Mia again. So I held on, and so did Laura, until with a sudden jolt that ripped us from the creature's back, we landed.

The snow was soft and powdery, about six inches deep, but lay atop a hard crust. We went through both, and also through another foot or so of snow beneath it. I struggled as the cold snow that sifted to fill the hole I'd created covered me. I managed to sit up and pull off my snow-encrusted glasses just in time to see the Krampus monster, which had turned to look at us, turn away, still clutching a screaming, struggling Mia to its chest.

My earlier thought that it looked spider-like was premature. Or maybe it *had* looked like a spider and had changed again. Now it looked more like a flea, with a bulbous back end that Laura and I had ridden God only knew how far. Or rather, as if a centaur was part obscenely huge flea and part bigfoot and part goat and part any other thing it happened to want to be at the time. It now had ten limbs: four shaggy arms that still gripped Mia tightly, while the six legs that supported its body couldn't seem to decide between horse or insect.

With its back toward us, I could see a bleeding gash where some of its fur had been ripped away, along with some of its flesh. The bloody mess was still in my hand; somehow I'd gripped it so hard I'd ripped the flesh right off it. It didn't seem to notice.

"Mia!" Laura shouted.

"Mom! Help me! Help me, please!"

The strangely fluid muscles in the Krampus' legs tensed.

"We will!" I struggled to my feet. So did Laura, but it was too late. We couldn't reach the thing before it made its next move. "We'll find you!"

Then, hind legs kicking out against the snow-covered field, it leapt again.

And Mia was gone.

And we were alone.

And that's when the stink struck us.

The Krampus had smelled awful; we'd just been too focused on Mia to pay it any notice. It was like an unwashed animal that had been sprayed by a skunk after rolling in fox shit. And now *we* smelled of it. Any part of our clothing that had been in contact with it had absorbed a little of the miasma, but our gloves, of course, were worse. And worst of all was my right glove, holding the bloody scrap of Krampus hide.

Gagging, I threw it away from me and tried to wipe the stench off in the snow, with only limited success.

"What do we do now?" Laura asked.

I had no answer.

Calling the police was not a possibility. Not only would they disbelieve our outlandish story, but wherever we'd ended up, there was no cell signal. We were standing on a perfectly flat snow-covered field under an overcast sky. There was just enough moonlight filtering through the clouds that we could see the hulking shadows of the mountains in front of us and to either side, surrounded by dense forests. Behind us was a dark valley. Wherever we were, not only was there no cell service, there were no lights at all. No streetlights, no lights filtering through window curtains. No cars winding through the mountain roads or the valley. It was as if we were the only people here, the only people who had *ever been here*. The two of us, and our daughter. And that thing.

"Turn off your phone," I suggested. "Save the battery." Because even if we had brought chargers with us, there was sure as hell nowhere to plug them into.

Laura nodded and powered down her phone. I did the same.

"Sam. That mountain, on the left. Does it look familiar to you?"

I shrugged. Mountains were fine, but you've seen one, you've seen them all.

"I'm serious. That's Mondseeberg. Our Gasthaus is right about... there." She pointed halfway up the dark mound. "*Should* be, I mean. And ahead of us is Drachenwand. I'm sure of it. I'd recognize that cliff face anywhere."

Whether it was Drachenwand or some other mountain with a cliff, that was where the Krampus was heading. It would be a long walk, and the question arose—what if we deviated, and never found the Krampus' next landing spot? We could walk off in a slightly wrong direction forever.

"Okay," I said. "I'm going to turn my phone on. It's got a compass. We can get a good reading and make sure we stay on track."

Laura nodded. "Make sure you put it on airplane mode," she said, unnecessarily.

"You think there are any airplanes here?" Nevertheless, I set it for airplane mode, and turned off wifi, and closed every app that allowed me to close it.

I pulled up the compass app and got a good reading, and then checked it again before Laura could tell me to.

"Wait," I said. I trudged over to the scrap of Krampus flesh and picked it up. Folding it bloody side in, I stuffed it into my coat pocket.

Laura wrinkled her nose. "Ick. Why?"

"Dunno, just a hunch. We don't know what we might need, if... when we find Mia."

"Yeah, okay," Laura said, in the tone of voice that meant the opposite.

But she didn't stop me, and she took my (other) hand when I offered it.

And then, hand in hand, Laura and I began the long trek toward the dark shape that eerily resembled the stark cliffs of Drachenwald.

Fortunately, there was little wind, or we might not have made it. Neither Laura nor I were what you might call outdoorsy types, and we quickly realized that we weren't equipped for this kind of weather. Our jackets, at least, were warm, but our gloves were inadequate, and our jeans were quickly encrusted with snow that got up under our pants legs and down into our boots. And while the crust under the powder was usually quite strong, every once in a while I'd find a spot not quite sturdy enough for my weight, and I'd drop through all the way up my thighs. Annoying the first few times, but it became harder and harder to climb out as time went by.

We had been walking about forty-five minutes when we got confirmation we were on the right path. The Krampus had left a large crater in the snow where it had landed, and once again we identified the direction of the next leap by the scoring of the creature's legs against the ice.

"Measure twice, trudge once," I muttered. It felt like my lips were cracking every time I talked. My nose was running from the cold and freezing on my face, and the tips of both my nose and ears were so cold they were burning.

We found the next landing spot about forty-five minutes later, but after that, they came farther apart. Not, I don't think, because the Krampus was leaping farther, but because we were slowing down. Each step became more and more difficult, and occasionally one of us would stumble. I had an image of us as wind-up dolls, slowly winding down, until we just... stopped.

"We're almost there," Laura said. "Get up. Keep walking."

I'd fallen through the crusty surface again, and after dragging myself out, just sat there on my knees, unable to muster the will to keep going.

"Ten minutes and we'll be off this damned ice. If you stop, you die. And then I die. And then Mia dies."

So, get up.

I got up.

I kept walking.

There was another snow crater not far from the forest's edge, and from there, footprints. No longer insect-like, the Krampus had assumed the shape of something with wide-splayed hooves.

"Reindeer," Laura said. "It's got reindeer feet, now."

"Yeah, okay."

"I'm serious!"

This was a terrible time for a marital spat, but between stress and exhaustion, it seemed inevitable.

"Like you're some damned reindeer expert?"

"You don't do as many Christmas events as I have without knowing what reindeer tracks look like. They're freaking weird, and they look like that, only smaller."

The tracks, monstrous reindeer or not, led to the edge of the forest, and we followed.

There was only one problem.

The snow settled atop the dense canopy of evergreen trees. Not below it. Below it was only darkness, deep and impenetrable. A thick carpet of pine needles covered the ground. Frozen together, they formed a spongy surface that cushioned footfalls and returned quickly to its prior form.

Maybe there was a trail a skilled tracker could find. But that was a talent neither Laura nor I possessed. Unless the Krampus dragged its feet—something it hadn't done in the snow—the trail ended here.

We argued, of course. If we used the flashlight on the phone we'd run out of charge faster. So, what did we want to do, just stand here at the edge of the forest and freeze with some charge left? What course was there, really, but to move forward.

The flashlight illuminated more shadows than trees. Once we got past the edge where a tiny bit of light still got in, there was very little by way of undergrowth. No bushes or thorn-covered brambles, like I remembered from my childhood, running around the woods near our house in the 'burbs.

We did crazy things, me and the other kids in the neighborhood, and we'd come home all scratched and scraped, clothes torn, skinned knees. Missing shoes, one or both lost in the mud we'd sometimes sink into up to our knees. Bruises from falling out of trees or down embankments. Catching snakes and salamanders and frogs and bringing them home in our coat pockets but forgetting about them until we heard Mom scream. And somehow, *somehow* not dying.

I felt that I'd used up all my spare lives as a kid, and this time I wouldn't be so lucky. We'd walk into the dark woods. We'd get lost, wander forever until we walked off a cliff. Or got eaten by a bear.

After all, without a trail to follow, what hope was there?

Laura interrupted my lamentations.

"What's that?"

"What's what?

"That! Over there!" She pointed. "Something shiny."

I panned the flash around a bit and saw it for myself. We approached, and Laura picked it up out of the pine needles.

Oh, Mia! My clever, clever girl.

It was a coin.

A five-schilling piece. Pre-euro currency. Cheap-ass Mondsee Krampuses weren't even giving out real money. Or rather, it was real money, but hadn't been legal tender for decades, just what they found in their piggy banks from when *they* were kids.

Still, it was exactly the kind of breadcrumb we needed.

Also, it meant that our girl was still alive, and in good enough condition to think through a problem.

Another also: it meant that she'd heard our promise to save her. If we failed to live up to that, we'd never hear the end of it.

We pressed on.

A little distance away we found another coin, this one a pale, brassy fifty-groschen piece. There was no third coin nearby, but we were able to take a compass reading based on the line those two points defined, and off we went.

The next pair of coins was a brassy one-schilling coin and a silvery ten-schilling, and kept us on roughly the same trajectory. The pair following that consisted of another five-schilling piece and a hard bon-bon in a golden foil wrapper. The Krampus had changed direction here, still heading south, but bearing a little more west than before.

"'Follow the money,' the detectives say," Laura muttered, half under her breath, "but I never realized how literally they meant it."

At some point, my phone died. Laura got hers out and did all the things: airplane mode, close all unnecessary apps, and so on. And we continued.

While the ice field had been perfectly flat, we'd been going gradually uphill since entering the forest. Now the incline became more noticeable. Sometimes on the steeper climbs, we could see where the Krampus hooves had dug into the carpet of pine needles, leaving divots that helped confirm we were on the right path. Mia was growing more frugal in her breadcrumb trail, leaving longer spaces between markers, and only dropping them when the Krampus changed direction. I hoped that she didn't run out before they ended up wherever the Krampus was taking her.

It wasn't a concern I wanted to state out loud. Out loud would make it more real. Out loud would make Laura as freaked as I was. She probably already was, but as long as neither of us voiced it, we could each contain our growing terror and pretend that we were sparing the other.

❖◦◦⬦◆⬦◦◦❖

Laura's phone was down to twenty percent charge and our pockets full of coins and candy when the trail brought us out of the forest and to a cliff face. And in the cliff ran a crack, wide enough for both of us to walk in side-by-side. The ground there was hard-packed earth, well-trod; even a suburban-to-urban transplant like me could recognize that. What it meant, I couldn't say. But we were soon to find out.

Laura pushed in front of me, leaving me to chase behind, whispering frantically as I tried to see through my suddenly fogged glasses.

"Wait! We don't know what's in there!"

"Yes, we do," she snarled. And of course, she was right—along with the sudden warmth inside the mountain came a concentrated stench of Krampus. And where Krampus was, that was where Mia would be.

But I was also right—we didn't know if there were others. Other Krampuses. Or other creatures. It seemed to me that the ground at the entrance to the cave was too well trafficked for a single creature, no matter how many legs it had.

But we'd come this far, this close. And Mia needed us. So, Laura rushed onward.

We climbed some rough-hewn stairs that wound through layers of rock we'd have found fascinating in other circumstances. Then the path dropped away before us—more steps, going down now, but deeper and wider. Built for something larger than us.

Each of these steps was a drop of about five or six feet. Fortunately, there seemed to be foot-and-handholds carved into them on one side, and we were able to get down without twisting our ankles or knees, or breaking any bones. They'd also be convenient on our way out. If we ever got out.

That seemed to be a shortcoming of our rescue plan that neither Laura nor I had discussed. *One* of the shortcomings. We also had no idea how to defeat the Krampus. But even if we did, what would we achieve other than dying here together, as a family?

I pushed the thought out of my head. We'd figure out how to die together *after* we figured out how to *be* together.

If Mia was even still alive.

The cave floor evened out as it continued to wind deeper into the mountain. Then suddenly, as we turned a corner, we glimpsed light ahead. Along with the light came the stench of the Krampus and the scent of burning flesh and hair.

Laura began to run. And again, I chased after her.

Chapter 3
Krampushöhle

WE BURST OUT OF THE TUNNEL AND INTO A LARGE CAVERN. THE Krampus's lair was lit by torches and a large fire. The Krampus itself was hunched before the fire, which cast its hideous shadow dancing against the wall to our right.

Something — or someone — was on the fire and burning, half obscured by the Krampus's bulk. The body was blackened, and it sizzled and popped as its skin crisped and fat melted into the flames.

I clamped a glove over Laura's mouth just as she started to scream Mia's name.

Not fast enough; the Krampus turned sharply.

I pulled Laura back into the tunnel. Had the Krampus seen us? The answer was probably not — it turned out the Krampus was relatively shortsighted — but we didn't know that at the time. It didn't really matter, though. We heard it sniff, then sniff more deeply. And then we heard it move.

I hazarded a peek around the tunnel's edge.

The good news? Mia was alive, still clutched possessively to the Krampus's chest.

The bad news? Sniffing the air deeply, the Krampus was following our scent directly toward us.

Smaller figures scattered out of its way.

As I watched, the Krampus grew two additional limbs, limbs that ended in long, sharp-looking claws.

"It's coming!" I hissed.

There was no way we could outrun it. The high, vertical steps, especially, would slow us down. Krampus, obviously, would not have that problem.

"We run in and split up," Laura said, optimistically. "One of us distracts the monster while the other one rescues Mia."

"Better idea," I said, fetching the scrap of Krampus pelt out of my pocket. I rubbed it all over her face as she shrieked. If the Krampus didn't know we were here yet, it knew it now. Never mind that, though, because it already knew we were here. I rubbed the fur on Laura's face and hair. On her jacket and pants, front and back, and on both her boots and gloves. "At least, I hope it's a better idea."

Laura spluttered, blinking away tears. "Oh my god."

Just then, the Krampus peered into the tunnel.

"This better work," Laura grumbled, and then stepped right in front of its face while I cowered deeper in the tunnel.

"Mom?" Mia sounded shocked. Like she didn't expect us to actually come through for her.

Laura didn't respond. She just stood in the entrance to the tunnel and blocked the Krampus's entrance. The Krampus sniffed again deeply. It nudged her with its nose and licked her face. Laura whimpered but didn't back down. But the Krampus did. I'm not sure what it was thinking, but it seemed satisfied that Laura wasn't an intruder. Maybe it thought that she was part of itself, some part that had come loose and then followed it home. Whatever its reasoning, it backed out of the tunnel and returned to the fire, taking a screaming Mia with it.

It was my turn to get a Krampus-hide rubdown. Laura seemed to take particular relish in smearing it over my face, laughing as I gagged on the horrific stench. I had curled my lips over my teeth and clamped down tight, but that didn't stop the long fur going up my nostrils.

But as disgusting as it was, I didn't mind. Both Laura and I seemed in a better place, emotionally. After all, we'd found a way to protect ourselves from the Krampus's notice, which was just a bonus over the real win: Mia was still alive and, as far as we could see, unharmed. And not a burning husk roasting over the coals of a fire.

Emboldened, we re-entered the room.

And found ourselves the objects of attention of every creature in the room *other* than the Krampus.

There were dozens of them, boys and girls, men and women of all ages. To be fair, not very many were actually terribly old. Only two were older than middle-aged, and from what we could tell, only a handful had reached middle-age itself. They wore a combination of animal hides and bits of repurposed clothing, patched together like quiltwork. One of the girls was nursing a baby. A couple of toddlers played together in the dirt that covered the floor. Some were standing; others were seated, either on the floor or on wooden logs, or on the stumps of stalagmites that had been broken off and then chiseled smooth. Smooth-ish.

From the look of it—and probably the smell of it, though *anything* would be hard-pressed to compete with the Krampus's stench—none of them had seen a bar of soap in years.

One of them, a man I'd have guessed to be in his thirties, rose from his stalagmite chair and approached us. He was dressed all in animal skins—a deerskin doublet that extended nearly to his knees and a pair of deerskin leggings. The leather itself had been inexpertly tanned.

Ignoring Laura, he stood facing me, looking me up and down. Then he spoke.

In German, of course. The only word I understood was "Krampus." I looked at Laura, who seemed rather put out at being ignored.

"He said you're pretty old for Krampus to take you for a plaything." Then she responded to the man, also in German. And then to me: "I told him Krampus didn't take us. It took our daughter and we've come to get her back."

The man looked sad, his gaze shifting from Laura to me and back to Laura. He spoke again, and Laura responded.

"He said he is sorry, but none who come here ever leave. We would have been better to stay home and make another child. Can you believe he said that? I told him that was bullshit and we'd find a way. We found our way here, and we'll find our way back out."

"But we don't even know where 'here' is."

Laura turned with a retort on her lips, a retort that remained unspoken as the Krampus chose that moment to move.

Krampus rose to its full height. Mia screamed as it lifted her over its head, nearly high enough for her to touch the cavern's roof. It whistled some sort of horrible, gurgling noise and leapt out into the middle of the cavern, where people scattered to avoid being trampled. It almost smashed Mia into a stalactite, missing it by inches. I noticed that a number of the stalactites had been broken off, probably in just this way.

Reaching down, Krampus snatched someone up off the ground.

That person didn't scream. Turns out this was pretty normal in the Krampus household.

Shrinking visibly, Krampus set Mia and the other person down on the ground, facing each other. It shrank some more and settled down on its haunches. To watch. It gazed out at them with obvious anticipation.

The person facing Mia was a boy, about Mia's size. He was wearing the remains of a puffy red snow-suit, cut apart and extended with strips of deer hide. I assumed it had fit him, once upon a time, but he'd grown at least a foot in height since then.

Mia extended her hand. "Mein Name ist Mia. Kannst du Englisch sprechen?"

The boy punched her in the face.

The Krampus giggled and clapped its hands as Mia fell back on her butt, clutching her nose. There was red on her gloves and smeared on her face. Blood dripped from her nose.

Laura and I jumped to intervene, but the man who had approached us gripped us both by the arm to hold us back. He was extremely strong. He said something in German and Laura snarled a response, but stopped struggling.

The boy stood there, shouting at Mia. In German. Laura didn't translate.

He should have been terrified. The look on Mia's face terrified *me*, and I wasn't the one fighting her. And maybe he was, but he kept shouting at her, and Krampus kept giggling and clapping in delight.

Mia pulled off her blood-stained mittens and dropped them in the dirt beside her. She got to her feet with her fists up in front of her.

Grinning, the boy lifted his fists.

Mia pulled one fist back to her ear. The boy raised his arms to block the punch and failed to block Mia's kick.

Clutching his groin, the boy doubled over. Mia grabbed his head and smashed her knee into his face.

The boy went down and didn't get up.

Krampus squealed with delight and jumped up and down.

One of the older men lifted the boy by the armpits and dragged him away, as he groaned pitifully.

Krampus reached an impossibly long arm out and snatched up another opponent for Mia. This one was significantly taller than Mia, a girl in her older teens, as far as I could tell. She had long, unkempt hair and a feral grin. She spread her arms wide, like an invitation to hug.

Mia wasted no time, launching herself at her opponent. She hit shoulder to midriff, setting the girl back on her heels. The girl took a step back to recover her balance, and then, with her height advantage, reached over Mia's shoulder and punched her from behind, hitting her in the kidney twice in rapid succession.

Mia pushed away from her, falling backward and crab-walking to get away. The girl gave a crooked smile and spread her arms again. When Mia didn't stand back up on her own, Krampus gripped her by the neck and pulled her up.

From the corner of my eye, I could see Laura seething, but the man held us firmly, and neither of us fought to break free.

Mia approached the girl again, more cautiously this time. It didn't matter. The girl stepped in and grabbed Mia's hair, using it to hold her in place while she hit her. She slapped her, punched her in the face and stomach and chest, while Mia swung punches and kicks that never connected.

The girl only stopped when Mia's attacks faltered and her knees buckled. Only then did she release Mia's hair, letting our girl collapse on the filthy dirt floor.

One of the men rose to collect her, but the man holding us released his grip and said something I didn't understand. But Laura did, and ran down to Mia's side. I took only a second or two to catch on, and reached Mia nearly as quickly. I gathered her up in my arms and with Laura fussing at my side, carried her away from the fighting ground.

Krampus didn't give us a second look.

But that didn't mean it had tired of its amusements. Now it grabbed another person to fight for its pleasure. This one was a boy, roughly of the same age as the girl who'd pummeled Mia into senselessness. He was tall, with long, blond hair, and was just as filthy as his opponent. This time, it was his turn to smile, while the girl glowered at him.

As the two faced off, circling each other warily, an older woman approached us and handed us a wet rag. It wasn't what I would call clean, but I suppose it was as clean as you got in Krampus's lair. It didn't smell like anything other than water, so Laura used it to dab the blood from Mia's face. Her nose was bloodied but not broken, and one eye was blackening. She would have bruises, certainly, but nothing looked life-threatening.

In the arena, the boy reached out a hand and touched the girl's cheek. Snarling, she slapped it away and followed with a series of punches, all of which he deflected. Again, he reached out to touch her cheek. This time, she grabbed his wrist and sank her teeth into his forearm.

He hissed his pain, but he didn't fight her, not then, and not when she hooked her leg behind his knees and shoved him to the ground. And again not when she threw herself on top of him.

This bout lasted significantly longer than the previous fights and went a good ways toward explaining how the babies in the cavern had come about.

Krampus treated it no differently from any of the other fights, clapping and giggling like some massive, horrible idiot child seeing bubbles for the first time.

I, for one, was glad Mia was too insensible to witness it. Laura snorted derisively.

"You think she's never been on the Internet before?"

I suppose there are certain types of innocence that are gone from the world forever.

We were spared any further of Krampus's amusements by the realization that dinner had finished roasting. I was relieved to see that the creature that had been crisping on the fire had hooves at the end of each long, skinny limb. Krampus snatched the deer out of the fire in a shower of sparks.

It occurred to me then to wonder at the fact that we hadn't all died of carbon monoxide poisoning. Turns out it was nothing magical; there was a hole in the cavern ceiling that let the smoke escape.

Krampus reached long-clawed fingers into the deer's carcass and split it open. It buried its face in the deer and slurped at the hot, bubbling entrails like it was a particularly gruesome bowl of ramen. It used its fingers to scoop out anything it missed—heart, bits of lung and offal—until the soft innards were all gone. It tossed the rest of the carcass aside.

The human residents of the lair descended on it like jackals.

It didn't take long for it to be stripped down to the bones. The man who'd spoken to us earlier—and perhaps saved our lives—approached with four strips of meat, three of which he handed out to us. He sat in the dirt and joined our first meal in our new home.

He introduced himself as Nikolaus, and said that he was the first. The first one Krampus took. The first plaything. And for a time, the only plaything. But Krampus gets bored. He likes new things to play with, and once a year, when the portal to our world opens, Krampus ventures out to find its next victim.

No, I'm sorry. Time muddles things. He didn't tell us all that right then. He told us his name, and he hinted that he might be much older than he looks. The rest came later, as he grew to know us better. At the time, he concentrated on milking us for information. How had we come here? When Krampus took Mia, how had we managed to follow? This was the first time in all the centuries that Krampus had been stealing children that a parent had come searching.

"We were close enough to see what was happening," Laura said, "even if nobody else seemed to notice. And when Krampus grabbed Mia, we grabbed Krampus, and then we were here. Wherever here is."

Nikolaus nodded. "That was stupid. Now you are all lost."

After the meal, Nikolaus gave us a quick tour. There wasn't much to see. Everyone lived in the big cavern. They slept where they liked, but seating was another matter. One didn't sit on someone else's stump or stalagmite unless you were invited. If you wanted a seat of your own, you needed to go out in the woods and get one yourself. If a seat became available (because the owner no longer needed it), it was offered to the oldest person who didn't already have one.

Another rule was that you didn't break Krampus's playthings. Krampus didn't like that. As a result, when there were personal conflicts, it was safest if people just worked it out, or if they couldn't, then avoided each other as much as possible.

The residents spoke a strange dialect of German that, according to Laura, was a creole of ancient and modern German, with a smattering of French, Italian, and southeast Balkan words and phrases. The children were taken from anywhere within the footprint of the Alps, and each added to the language as they learned it.

"For water you will need to make yourselves bowls," Nikolaus said. "You can share mine for now, if you refill it."

He took a torch and led us to a crevice in the side of the cavern. As we followed the tunnel, we heard the sound of running water. We ended up in a chamber through which a fast-running underground stream ran. Nikolaus pointed to side where the stream entered.

"On this side you get good water. Over there you make bad water."

By the cave wall a wooden toilet had been constructed, suspended over the water as it ran out of the room.

"Do not fall in," he said, as Mia leaned over to peer into the stream. "Is very deep. Very strong. Very cold. Never see you again."

And that was our first night in Krampushöhle.

Chapter 4
Das Längste Jahr

TIME MOVED SLOWLY IN KRAMPUSHÖHLE.

After a few weeks, Krampus became acclimated to our scents, so Laura and I no longer needed to rub ourselves down with the horrible, rotting bit of Krampusfleisch. We became part of Krampus's toybox, which came with its own set of problems.

We did what we needed to survive. Under Laura's tutelage, Mia and I managed to learn enough of this weird German dialect to get by. Mia learned faster than I did, of course, and pretty soon she was conversing pretty comfortably with the other kids.

During what passed for daytime in this world, when a sort of half-light filtered through the overcast sky and the temperature became marginally less bitter, the forest was less than impossibly dark, and people went out to forage. They dug under the pine needles for strange funguses, none of which killed us, but several of which took us on strange hallucinatory internal journeys of the sort that, in another life altogether, we'd recently warned Mia against. They gathered firewood, which they cut into manageable pieces with rough stone axes and hauled back to the cave to feed Krampus's fire. They also hunted small game with slings and stones or ad-hoc spears—rabbits and squirrels and the occasional songbird—which made for a nice, if guilty, change from burnt venison.

Krampus also ventured out to hunt, returning with a stag or doe clutched in some appendage. Twice or thrice it was a wild boar. In all cases, whatever was captured got thrown onto the fire, whether it was dead or not. Sometimes when Krampus would go out, it would not return that day, or for several days. Those were hungry times, and brought to mind a bit too vividly *Lord of the Flies* (William Golding, 1954), the film of which Mia had seen recently and from which I worried had taken all the wrong lessons.

Despite our combined predations, the forest teamed with life. This was, frankly, a surprise for Laura and me, for on our travels to the cave that first Krampusnacht we'd heard none of the sounds one might associate with the wilderness at night. No insects, no owls. Nothing rustling or scuttling through the branches or across the pine needle carpet. It was as if the forest had been stripped of every living thing. We weren't the only ones this spooked; in fact, *nobody* was willing to brave the forest at night. It was Nikolaus who explained it to us.

"There are things that prowl at night, and nothing or nobody that moves in the dark survives. Sometimes we find pieces of them."

"We didn't see anything like that," Laura said.

"This is why the people gave you wide berth at first. You survived the forest at night and faced down Krampus. They would not risk trying to make a plaything of you, like Krampus does of us."

We figured if something really was out there and it really was as dangerous as all that, it was probably the light from our cell phones that kept the mystery creatures away. But then, maybe it was just a tale told to keep people from running off.

Comfort was a rarity, living in a cave on a dirt floor. It's easy to see why cavemen decided to evolve into creatures that designed and utilized ergonomic office chairs.

One morning, Laura woke with a stiffer neck and back than usual, and when I asked her if she was okay, she snapped at me.

"If only I'd married someone *useful*. Like a carpenter."

Which might have sounded unfair, except that for the last five years, her professor's salary had kept my failing artisanal furniture workshop afloat. I'd subleased the workshop to someone with actual customers, and even before we'd gotten trapped in the Krampusnacht-mare before Christmas, I wasn't sure there would be any business left for me to return to. For all I know that was the real reason Laura took the position.

After Nikolaus helped me make a stone axe of my own, Laura and Mia and I went out into the forest to gather pine branches, which we stripped of needles and brought into the cavern. The thicker branches formed the frame of our wicker chairs and cots, and we wove the thinner branches together to form the seats and backs. Soon I was teaching everyone how to do it.

When the weather grew warmer, we joined the others foraging in the woods, bringing back whatever edible things we could find growing, and fishing in the lake. It took a lot of fish guts to feed a Krampus, but the clear, clean waters of the lake had no shortage of fish.

I also harvested the reeds that grew lakeside, which I soaked and split and wove into tatami-style mats. These gave us reasonably good cushions for our chairs and cots, and created a much-needed barrier between us and the persistent pine sap.

Even those who refused to give up their hard-earned stalagmite thrones — like Nikolaus — showed interest in the new mats.

And that is how we overcame the fear and reticence the others had for us.

I mentioned that Krampus's acceptance of Laura and me came with drawbacks. That became evident some days after we'd finally stopped masking ourselves with eau de Krampus. Laura and I were minding our business, watching Mia playing with the other kids — some sort of game with unintelligible and everchanging rules — when suddenly I felt hot clawed fingers wrap around my waist.

Krampus lifted me in the air and pulled me down in front of the fire to face off against one of the other men. The man lifted his fists.

He was older than I was, and both smaller and scrawnier, but his wiry frame hid a survivor's strength. The fight went longer than either of us expected, I think. I was bleeding from my nose and mouth and knuckles by the time he stopped fighting back. I didn't even notice the bite wounds until later. Krampus was over the moon with delight.

My next opponent was a woman, perhaps in her early twenties. Pregnant, just starting to show. Her name, I learned later, was Wiede. She gave me a hesitant smile and approached, reaching out to stroke my face. I looked at Laura and Mia, who watched me in horror, and pushed Weide away.

Frowning now, she tried again, pulling her deerskin shirt over her head and letting it drop at our feet. I tried not to look at her breasts. Once again she approached, and once again I pushed her away.

With a snarl, tenderness turned to fury. She kicked me in the knee and planted her own knee in my face when I dropped. Stunned, I offered no resistance as she knocked me to the dirt and proceeded to kick me into senselessness.

I couldn't tell you which bruise or laceration came from which of the fights, only that I came out of the event feeling like I had won both of them — the latter a moral victory.

That victory turned to ash in my mouth a few weeks later when Krampus chose Laura for its plaything.

Laura didn't like to fight.

She didn't.

I could feel Mia trembling with rage next to me, but I didn't dare look at her, for fear of what I might see in her eyes.

Or what she might see in mine.

One day, while out foraging for food, a boy named Martin fell from a tree. He'd been reaching for eggs in a nest and lost his footing. Nikolaus and I set his broken arm as best we could and immobilized it with sticks and vines. More concerning was that one of the branches he'd fallen through had punctured his abdomen.

Over the next few days, Martin grew feverish, and stinking pus leaked from the wound. Other residents gathered around him, tending him, plastering his wound with strong-smelling astringent paste made from some leaves found by the lake. Later, I realized that they were shielding him from Krampus's attention.

"He needs a hospital," Laura said, to Nikolaus. "Or he's going to die."

Nikolaus nodded. "Yes, he will die."

Anger flashed across Laura's face. "Krampus knows how to get to our world. You *claim* you've been here a long time. Surely you know how he does it."

Nikolaus's gaze shifted from Laura to me and back again. Something in his eye was calculating. "Yes. There is a doorway, high in the mountain. It is only open once every year, on Krampusnacht. Martin will not live that long."

When Krampus went out to hunt that day, Nikolaus gathered some of the older residents. They produced a wooden stretcher, on which they had placed one of my tatami mats. They laid Martin on it, then secured him with vines.

It was a somber procession through the caves, and to my surprise it ended at the underground stream from which we got our water.

As Nikolaus removed the restraints, the people processed through, each whispering something into Martin's ear and touching his fevered brow before moving on.

"Tell him what your greatest wish is," Nikolaus told Mia, when it was her turn, and indicated that we should follow suit.

Once everyone had had their turn, Nikolaus and one of the others approached the stretcher. In one swift motion, they lifted Martin and tossed him into the water.

The water was as swift as it was dark and cold, and Martin was gone.

Why? That's what we wanted to know.

Laura was apoplectic while I seethed silently.

"It is better than the fire," Nikolaus said. "Better for him. Better for us."

It took time to understand what he meant with that last phrase.

Mia figured it out first.

"Eww! Well, *I* wouldn't eat him."

"Then you would starve," Nikolaus said, "and then you would be next."

Mia opened her mouth to argue, then thought better of it.

Anyway, Martin was one year younger than Mia. He was the first boy Mia fought for Krampus's pleasure. He had been in Krampushöhle for three years. His last name was Fischer, and he had been taken from Mittenwald. In case his parents want to know.

By end of summer, Laura and I were barely speaking.

I'd tried talking to her once about her fight tactics.

"I'm a musician," she said. "I have to protect my hands. And my lips."

Turns out the only person she'd actually fight was me, when Krampus finally set us against each other. Maybe because she knew I wouldn't hit her. On the other hand, she didn't hold back. No "my hands are precious instruments." Not this time. I hadn't been aware how much anger and resentment she held for me. I mean, we'd been bickering and sniping at each other for years. That's what married couples did. But I'd have done anything for her. Even shut down my dream to let her follow hers. And if not for her, then for Mia.

I didn't understand what had just happened. When I said as much, Laura shook her head and walked away.

After that, I'd moved out of our shared cot. Slept on the dirt for a few days before I'd made a new one for myself. Mia came with me.

And for the most part, Laura and I lived as separate lives as we could, trapped in the same cavern. I tried to pretend she wasn't there at all, and I tried to pretend I didn't see how much time she was spending with Nikolaus.

But ignoring only goes so far. When she stabbed a hole in her thigh trying to do her own woodworking, Mia and I were both immediately at her side.

Laura had found a thick-walled reed about an inch and a half diameter, and she was trying to poke holes in it with a long, thin rock shaped vaguely like an ice pick. Which was now protruding from her leg.

I know enough about anatomy to know there's a super important artery in the thigh, but not enough to know if she was anywhere near it. I sent Mia to fetch some of the vines that we used as ropes, just in case, before we pulled it out. Fortunately, I didn't need to learn how to apply a tourniquet in real time. Blood ran, but didn't squirt.

Mia knew to start water boiling to sanitize bandages. After Martin's accident, we'd pitched the idea to Nikolaus and he'd sacrificed his stalagmite throne, chiseling the seat into a bowl and hollowing out the space below it for a fire. Not that it would have saved Martin, but smaller wounds had festered in the filth. I'd sacrificed both my shirt and undershirt for bandages and now wore the same stinking deerskin tunic that the others did.

In the meantime, I escorted Laura to the underground stream and proceeded to do my best to irrigate the wound to reduce the chance of infection setting in. Pants off, she sat at the edge of the stream with her leg extended as I scooped the cold water over the wound. It felt... odd... touching her bare skin for the first time in months. Simultaneously familiar and awkward. And into that awkwardness, I managed to say all the wrong things. Like:

"This was seriously stupid. What the fuck were you thinking?"

Laura turned and slapped at me, almost slipping into the water in the process. Not almost. I caught her as she was going in. And a good thing: after everything that had happened, Mia would never believe I hadn't pushed her.

"I did it for you," she said, when the danger was past. "And for Mia."

"Explain."

"I've been talking to Nikolaus a lot—"

"I've noticed."

Laura's eyes were daggers, but she continued. "And he thinks that Krampus can be distracted. He's seen Krampus get lost in music. Melodious music. There were times when he almost didn't make it back from his Krampusnacht trip because he got distracted by the music. That's why he only goes to places where there's no music, or the music is dissonant. That's why Krampusmuzik has dissonance. Like tritones. Or Locrian mode."

"I don't understand."

"On Krampusnacht, the portal will be open. Nikolaus knows where it is. If I can distract Krampus long enough, we can escape. We can save Mia."

I made dozens of instruments. More. I brought back heavy reeds and tree limbs that had potential for hollowing. I drilled them out and added finger holes where Laura indicated. Most of them were failures. A finger hole only needed to be a millimeter off to ruin the pitch.

In the meantime, Laura experimented with mouthpieces. She had me fashion recorder-style mouthpieces, where the sound was produced with air flowing over and past a lip carved into the mouthpiece itself, as well as mouthpieces designed to accommodate single or double reeds. Laura was proficient with all sorts of wind instruments, but her passion was oboe. She made reeds by the hundreds, throwing away almost all of them, looking for perfection.

In the end, the instrument she settled on consisted of three bodies lashed together and connected to a common mouthpiece. Each body was a different length—the central one was designed to drone on middle C, while the left and right were pitched an octave up and a third apart. I made different mouthpieces to accommodate different types of reeds, but I knew she would choose the double reed. In so many ways, Laura had revealed herself as a completely different person than the woman I'd believed I'd lived with for fifteen years, but at least this one thing I knew.

When it was done and Laura had tested it out in the privacy of the forest, she nodded with feigned indifference. "Well, at least it sounds better than a double reed slide music stand."

Laura played it in Krampus's presence once, to see how it reacted. It was as Nikolaus had said. Krampus tilted its head with befuddled fascination as the first crystal pure sounds filled the chamber—the introductory notes of Stravinsky's *Rite of Spring*. Krampus stood as if spellbound while Laura played, but *Rite of Spring* soon devolves into dissonance, so she segued into the solo from Mozart's *Oboe Concerto in C Major*, adapted, of course, to the peculiarities of this instrument.

When she was done, she quickly hid the instrument. Krampus shook itself, turning its head and blinking as if coming out of a stupor. And then it went out to hunt for the evening's meal.

After that, Laura only played the instrument when Krampus was not around.

"I don't want him getting used to it," she said.

Laura had taken up Nikolaus's habit of gendering Krampus as male. I saw no obvious indications, nor subtle ones, that it had any sexuality at all. Or even any awareness of sexuality. It seemed unable to differentiate between a fistfight and sex, and took delight in watching its animate toys "play" in whichever way it went.

By the time we had fashioned a suitable instrument for Laura's purposes, the days were growing short, and the weather was not the only thing that had grown chilly. Laura and I had worked closely together to build this thing, but we had bickered fiercely throughout the process, and once she had no further use for me, our interactions fizzled to nothing.

Wiede, the first woman Krampus had had me fight, had her baby. It was a difficult labor, her first, and she almost died. She still might have, had Mia and I not intervened. Krampushöhle did not breed compassion, and nobody else seemed willing to care for her and the child while she thrashed in fever. There was even talk of "taking her swimming," as we'd done with poor Martin, but I was certain (or at least hopeful) that she'd recover if we gave her a chance. I'm pleased to say I was right.

Laura, who had replaced my presence in her cot with Nikolaus, glowered when Wiede and her unnamed baby boy moved into my cot. To my surprise, Mia was cool with it.

"Just don't expect me to call her Mom," she said.

Mia was twelve now, and showing interest in boys. She'd had her first period, with all the accompanying difficulties of managing that in the environment we were in. I'd had to replace parts of the tatami mat we used for our mattress after the surprise of that first night.

I tried to have "The Talk" with her, but she was unreceptive.

"You don't want to get pregnant here," I said. "You saw how it went for Wiede, and it could have been much worse."

"We'll be out of here by then," Mia said, with more conviction than I felt.

But she didn't sleep with any of the boys, or the girls, either. I don't think it was out of a lack of interest, or a concern about the risk. I think it was because her parents would have been watching from the front row. And even in Krampus's lair, that was a pretty strong disincentive.

Chapter 5
Krampusnacht, Revisited

ALTHOUGH WE STILL WEREN'T SPEAKING, IT WAS OBVIOUS THAT Laura was getting progressively more tense as Krampusnacht approached, snapping peevishly at Nikolaus and anyone else who had the misfortune of venturing too close. Mia came to me in tears after Laura had reamed her out over some perceived failing. Wiede offered Mia the nipple that the baby wasn't currently using.

"Oh my *God*!" Mia shouted as she stomped off. "Is *everyone* here stupid?"

"What?" Wiede said. "It quiets the baby."

Wiede had been born in Krampushöhle, to a mother that had also been born there. Whatever residual sense of societal appropriateness remained with those whom Krampus had abducted did not trickle down to the native-born.

Laura was not alone in her anxiety, but I turned it inward, rather than outward. It manifested as disturbed sleep and obsessive whittling. I carved small sculptures, mostly busts, of the people there. I started with Laura, and then Mia, and Weide and Nikolaus. I tried one of Martin, but I'm not sure I got his features right. Mia liked it, though.

One day I found Mia holding the sculpture of Laura, turning it over in hands. She looked up at me.

"How can she be so strong and so weak at the same time? How can she be so angry and so sad and so full of hate and love all at the same time?"

"I don't know, kiddo."

"How did you ever love her?"

I sighed and sat next to Mia and held her close.

"I don't know that, either. But I did. And I still do."

"I hate her," Mia said.

I nodded and kissed her on the temple. "But don't forget to love her, too."

And then it was here. Krampusnacht. Or the day before the night, rather.

It wasn't clear that Krampus was aware of what day it was. Maybe it only knew when the portal opened, at dusk. Nikolaus confirmed that that seemed possible. That was a wrinkle that might throw the plan askew. Which would be the stronger call for Krampus's attention? Laura's music? Or the portal?

Midway through the day, Laura cornered me in the room with the underground stream.

"What are you doing?" I asked, as she backed me up against the cave wall.

She answered with a kiss, as fierce as our worst arguments.

We made love there, atop the tangle of our clothes. Fierce as the kiss, and then tenderly, and then fiercely again, and only tangentially aware of the people coming in to access the stream. We'd both have bruises, I was sure.

After, as we dressed, Laura caught my eye.

"Follow the plan. Get Mia out. And the others. But Mia first, that's the most important thing. I'll be right behind you."

"Promise?"

She answered with a kiss, long and sweet and tender and full of a promise that I didn't understand at the time.

As night fell, Krampus roused from its place by the fire, wicked intent showing on its hideous face.

Laura put the instrument to her lips. Wet the reed.

The first notes danced out, languid and mournful. Stravinsky again. Krampus froze.

Laura played the phrase through to just before the first hint of dissonance and then repeated da capo, several times.

Krampus stretched and flowed, its body undulating to the music.

We had filled a wooden bowl with water for Laura, along with a wooden cup, to help her keep playing, and she had a good dozen spare reeds at hand. She had been practicing whenever Krampus was off hunting to teach her lips and fingers how to play the pieces on this instrument, and blowing the reed by itself to build up her lips for this marathon performance.

Laura shifted to Mozart.

"Now," Nikolaus instructed.

Mia and I trailed Nikolaus out of the cavern, and the rest of the cavern's residents followed. Some, like Wiede, who had never known another world than this, had shown some trepidation, but in the end everyone joined us.

Krampus didn't notice our departure.

The passage to the portal took us first through the tunnel system that led to the underground stream but branched off through a crevice set high in the wall that was barely wide enough for the largest of us to squeeze through. There was no way Krampus could fit, unless it could make its bulk flow like an octopus. I didn't want to think about it. (I thought about it.)

Laura's music followed us like a ghost, slowly losing coherence. The cave echoed each note dozens of times, and echoed the echoes, until Mozart sounded like early Pink Floyd. The echoes bridged the breaks, for breath, or for water.

This new tunnel system was far more challenging than the one that led to the stream, which had been chipped away by the residents for hundreds of years. By the time we reached the end of the tunnel, my hands and knees and shins were scraped raw and bloody, and I'd lost track of how many times I'd brained myself on an outcropping rock or stalactite. All of us were coughing from the rank smoke issued by the torches we bore. There were not many, just enough that we were not in absolute darkness. Still, Laura's notes followed us, and the smoke seemed almost like their physical incarnation.

The end of the tunnel terminated in a ragged wall on which flashed images. Dozens, hundreds, more, superimposed on each other. There were people and torches and lights and people dressed like Krampus, cars and buildings and roasted chestnut carts. Too much and too fast for me to make sense of.

Nikolaus stopped in front of the portal.

"There is something you must know, Samuel. Before you go. Because you must make a choice now."

"I thought we'd already made the choice to leave."

Nikolaus sighed. "I have said before, I was the first. I said this because I *was* the first. A thousand years, maybe. I do not know how many. Krampus took me in the night and brought me to his lair, and there he played with me. And it should have stayed there, just Krampus and me. But loneliness is hard for a boy. So Krampus found me someone to play with."

"Does..."

Nikolaus pressed dirty fingers to my lips.

"They did not live very long, these children. Too weak. Too *good*. Not until I helped. I will show you."

He stared into the kaleidoscope of images for a few moments and then the images stilled, resolving into a single scene. The central square of a small town. Not Mondsee. Nikolaus pointed at a boy of about eight.

"This boy here. See how fierce he is? See how he faces the whip with defiance? See how he faces those around him with disregard?"

"You'd choose him because he's an asshole?" Mia said.

"Yes, but not just because. Look here. His parents. See how they hold their bodies? Apart from each other, and their attention more like knives at each other's throats than on their child? Yes, that is the child I would choose for Krampus. His parents? With nothing remaining to hold them together, everything they are together is dust. If they choose, they can move on and find new lives. Perhaps they can even find happiness. That is my gift."

"Wait. You're saying that *you* chose me? Not Krampus?" Mia stared at him with an incredulity I wish I felt. I'd always known that in some way we were unable to fix, we were letting Mia down.

"And you chose me *because my parents suck*? You should die!"

Nikolaus smiled at her pityingly. "Child, I have tried." He turned to me. "Now, it is time for you to choose. Where will you go?"

The wall had returned to its dizzying collage.

It was hardly a choice. I only knew one small Alpine town. The Marktplatz stuttered into view, with its zigzag marble tiles and unmistakable buttery yellow basilica.

"Go," I told Mia.

"Not without you."

"I promised your mom. Save you first, then everyone else. Take Wiede and the baby with you."

Mia hugged me tightly enough that my focus on the portal wavered, and the image of Mondsee's Marktplatz with its torches and horse-riding Krampuses and terrified, crying children wavered as well.

"I love you, Dad."

It was the first time in years she'd said that. She took Wiede's hand and stepped through the portal. I saw them appear in the square, as the horses shied suddenly away from them. One of the Krampuses lost his seat and fell hard on the cobblestone. I was too thrilled to care.

In small clusters, the residents of Krampushöhle stepped into the portal and appeared in Mondsee. The stolen children cheered, hugged each other and horrified strangers, some literally leaping with joy; the native-born clustered together, looking around furtively. I couldn't blame them. They'd never seen so much as a mud hut, and now they were surrounded by multistory buildings and strange people and stranger smells. Still, the people filed through the portal when their turn came, until it was only Nikolaus and me.

And Laura's music, the strains filtering through the tunnels and echoing with odd reverberations.

"Go, now," Nikolaus said.

"Not without Laura."

"She did not tell you? No, I suppose she would not. This is the deal we made: Mia goes home, Laura stays with me. The rest of you? I do not care." He turned away from me, and from the portal, and began the trek back to Krampus's cavern. To Laura. "Go," he said.

"She said she'd be right behind us. Right behind me."

He turned to look at me and slowly shook his head.

And then I was alone.

Behind me, the portal flickered and flashed, while Laura's music surrounded me.

I waited for her.

I waited while the music shifted back to Stravinsky.

I waited until the portal started to fade, before I fixed it back on Mondsee. I stepped through into an almost empty town square.

A police car door opened and an officer approached me.

"Come," she said, in a German that sounded weirdly stilted to my ears. "I will take you to your daughter."

Chapter 6
St. Nick's Gift

I SUPPOSE IT'S REASONABLE THAT IT WOULD TAKE A LONG TIME TO untangle decades worth of missing children all reappearing at once, along with a couple dozen literally undocumented people. Still, it didn't *feel* reasonable, and Mia was incensed that our house had been packed up and sold in our absence, and many of our belongings auctioned or sent to landfill. My parents and Laura's had kept some things that they felt were sentimental, and some of Mia's clothes and toys. The clothes didn't fit, and in a sense, neither did the toys.

I remember Mia cutting open a box pulled from storage and pulling things out with growing horror.

"Who *was* I?" she said.

Good question. Who were any of us, anymore?

For the last four years, Wiede and her son, Felsblock, had been living with us, but it looked like their visas might not be renewed next year, and Wiede didn't seem committed enough to fight for it. We'll miss them, of course, but she's a feral one, Wiede is, and I always knew that whatever it was we had together was temporary.

Why "Felsblock"? Because the Austrian authorities required that she name the child—the tradition in Krampushöhle was that the kids would name themselves, when they felt they found the right one. Felsblock is German for boulder, which, Wiede says, is what he felt like coming out. He can change it later when he thinks of something more fitting.

A crime reporter in Austria interviewed us for a piece on the Krampusnacht disappearances. Her research showed that, scattered across the Alpine region, there had been a child lost every year. But not the year we returned, and not any Krampusnacht since then. That's only four Krampusnachts, but it might just be the start of a pattern.

Of course, it means something different to Mia and me than to anyone else. It means that Laura is still alive, still playing Stravinsky and Mozart to a rapt audience of one. And so we scour the crime reports every year, hoping and praying to find nothing.

December's coming quick. Soon, we'll be getting on a plane, for the reunion. Every year we gather in a large cavern in central Austria. Of course, we have to be environmentally sensitive. No bonfires. Electric lanterns instead of torches. We bring lawn chairs and blankets and warm clothes. We put tarps down before spreading topsoil for the arena and clean up when we're done. Leave no trace.

There's a hat, and names scribbled on slips of paper.

And then we fight. Or whatever.

This year, Mia seems extra nervous.

"I'm not nervous, Dad," she says, when I say something, and her face colors. "It's just, I was thinking that maybe I might not fight. I mean, not every time."

"Oh?"

"I mean, it depends on who it is!" And then, "Forget it, forget I said anything."

"Okay, duly forgotten." No doubt she knows exactly who it will be and has figured a way to rig the pick. I muss her hair. "Just one thing. If you promise to be careful, I'll promise to close my eyes."

Because as far as scary things that a father might face regarding his daughter, this barely rates.

Besides, it was Krampusnacht, and none of the regular rules applied.

About the Author

MUCH TO HIS EMBARRASSMENT, BERNIE MOJZES HAS OUTLIVED Lord Byron, Percy Shelley, Janice Joplin, and the Red Baron, without even once having been shot down over Morlancourt Ridge. Having failed to achieve a glorious martyrdom, he has instead turned his hand to the penning of prose, an example of which you currently hold in your hands. Or is perhaps being projected from an electronic device perched atop your stationary bicycle or treadmill as a distraction from such mundane, repetitive tasks. Since undertaking this labor, he has had a small bushel of short stories published in anthologies and various online venues (37 when he stopped counting in 2014), and has himself published the now-defunct online zine, *Unlikely Story*, and edited two anthologies: *Clowns: The Unlikely Coulrophobia Remix*, and *The Flesh Made Word*. His first full-length endeavor, *Mistress of Bees*, was released in 2025 (and he does very much hope you'll read it (even though he hasn't managed to put it on his long out-of-date website, www.kappamaki.com (which he has been failing to update for many years — maybe someday that will change.)))

About the Artist

LINDA SABOE IS AN ARTIST WORKING IN GRAPHITE, COLORED PENCIL, paint, and clay. As a nature lover, most of her art and photography is centered on animals, domestic and wild, and fantastic beasts that sometimes visit her space, changing it in strange and subtle ways.

Linda resides in the western suburbs of Philadelphia with her husband (and love of her life), Bernie Mojzes, along with various critters who show up from time to time.

To see more of her work, please visit http://croneswood.com.